JAMIE

AND THE

WHIPPERSNAPPER

ENID RICHEMONT

ILLUSTRATED BY GRAHAM SMITH

RED FOX

For Alfie with love

A Red Fox Book

Published by Random House Children's Books
20 Vauxhall Bridge Road, London SW1V 2SA

A division of The Random House Group Ltd
London Melbourne Sydney Auckland
Johannesburg and agencies throughout the world

1 3 5 7 9 10 8 6 4 2

First published in Great Britain by
Red Fox in 2000

Printed and bound in Denmark by Nørhaven A/S

Papers used by Random House Group Ltd are natural,
recyclable products made from wood grown in sustainable forests.
The manufacturing processes conform to the
environmental regulations of the country of origins.

The Random House Group Limited Reg. No. 954009

www.randomhouse.co.uk

ISBN 0 09 940098 7

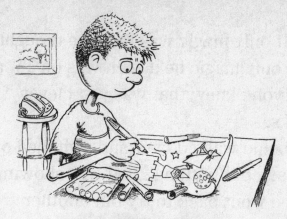

CHAPTER ONE

Jamie was trying out his new felt tips.
He made a big purple sky and a round,
cheesy moon. He drew a goggle-eyed
wizard in a magic castle, and a witch
on a broomstick and a man on a horse.

'I could be the man,' Jamie decided.
'But I'd have better magic than the
wizard or the witch. I'd make things
really happen – turn that dinner lady
who picks on us into a duck. Get
miserable Mr Biggins to give my school
his messy old field. Or even make my
dad a bit less grumpy.

3

'If only magic was real,' he thought. The only magic he'd seen was on TV, and everyone knew that was just clever tricks.

Jamie walked over and switched on the set, but nothing good was showing. So he went back to try out another picture.

At the table, an egg now lay on Jamie's magic castle.

'Funny,' he thought. 'It wasn't there before.'

He picked it up. It was bigger than the eggs Mum usually bought. It was smooth and heavy, with faint gold and green speckles. How had it got there?

Mum came in. 'That must be one of my duck eggs,' she cried. 'Have you been mucking about?'

Jamie handed it over. 'I didn't put it there,' he said.

'Well it didn't fly there,' said Mum.

5

Jamie followed Mum out to the kitchen and watched her place his egg with three others in a bowl.

Jamie gawped at them. 'They're big,' he said. 'Are there baby ducks inside?'

'I hope not.' Mum grinned. 'I got these from the butcher. I asked him for three. He must have given me four.'

Jamie goggled. 'Can you eat them?'

'You bet,' said Mum.

'Don't they taste funny?' asked Jamie.

'They're delicious. They're scrummy. When your dad comes in, we'll have one each for supper.'

Jamie hoped she'd forget. He hoped Dad wouldn't want one.

But, 'Duck eggs?' Dad said when he saw them in the kitchen. 'I haven't had a duck egg since I was a boy.'

So Mum set a pot of water to boil on the stove. Then she picked up the egg Jamie'd found on his magic castle picture.

'**Aaah!**' she shrieked as, Bang! Crack! Sizzle! it exploded, and a Something flew out.

It had fluttery grey batwings and big golden eyes. It had a rainbow-coloured tummy and a knotted blue tail. It had a shiny black snout and pink fingers and toes, and it was very, very, very cross.

'Wicked!' it squawked, flying up to the ceiling.

'What the devil is it?' shouted Dad.

Mum grabbed hold of Jamie. 'Help!' she shrieked.

'What do you mean, help?' The Something snorted out puffs of white smoke. 'You're the ones who nearly boiled me alive!' it spat.

'We didn't know you were in there,' wailed Mum.

'Get back!' ordered Dad. 'I'll deal with this.' And he grabbed a strainer and scrambled into the sink.

'Careful!' called Mum. 'That creature might sting!'

Dad aimed, then leapt.

'Missed!' crowed the Something from the handle of a saucepan. 'Missed

again!' it squealed, swinging upside
down. 'Oh, give up,' it told Dad, taking
a bite of kitchen paper. 'Mmm,' it
sighed. 'This tastes good.'
Then it flew down and
settled on Jamie's shoulder.
'Get it off me!' yelled
Jamie.
Dad tried to swat it,
but it just went on sitting
there. Jamie suddenly
found he didn't really mind
it. It even felt warm and
snuggly against his neck.
'You're mine,' the
Something told him, nuzzling
his ear. 'Because you're the one
who called me.'
'No I didn't!' Jamie went
scarlet. 'I didn't call anyone!'
he cried.

CHAPTER TWO

'I suppose I'll have to stay,' declared the Something.

'Well, you can suppose something else!' roared Dad.

'Manners!' The Something ruffled its batwings. 'You lot nearly boiled me, don't forget. I could report you to your chief magician. You might end up as flu bugs, or spots on someone's nose!'

Dad shrugged. 'We haven't got a chief magician.'

'No chief wizard?' The Something wrinkled its snout. 'No wonder you're peculiar. No wonder you're strange.'

'We're just normal,' said Dad. 'And we don't need any magic. We've got cars and aeroplanes and computers and TV.'

'Whirligigs! Whirligigs!' The Something tossed its head scornfully. Then it flashed its eyes at Dad. 'So you don't believe in magic?'

'No I don't,' Dad laughed.

The Something rolled its golden eyes and turned a cartwheel in the air. Then it blinked once, twice, thrice, and Jamie's house disappeared.

'Ugh!' yelled Mum. 'I'm sitting in a mud hole!'

'Magic?' crowed the Something.

'Rubbish!' Dad said, struggling to get up. 'Must be a landslide,' he muttered.

'I want my supper,' grumbled Jamie.

'And it's starting to rain,' wailed Mum. 'And oh!' she squealed. 'I'm sure there's a worm down my neck!'

'Magic?' sang the Something, doing cartwheels in the air.

'Bring the house back,' begged Mum.

'He's got to ask me.' The Something pointed at Dad.

'So bring the house back,' growled Dad, shrugging. 'If you can.'

The Something puffed out white smoke rings. 'What's the missing word?' it demanded, hanging upside-down.

'Please, I suppose,' grunted Dad. And they were sitting in the kitchen.

'That's not possible,' Dad muttered, brushing leaf mould out of his hair.

'So can I stay?' the Something asked.

Mum sighed. 'It doesn't look as if we've got much choice now, does it?'

But Jamie was staring at the other eggs in the bowl. 'Do you have,' he gulped nervously, 'any brothers and sisters?'

'Not in your world.' The Something flew back to the shelf.

'So where's your world?' asked Jamie. 'Did you come in a spaceship?'

'Spaceships?' It tittered. 'More whirligigs.'

'What's a whirligig?' Jamie asked.

'Oh, you know.' The Something wiggled its ears. 'A thingummy. A whatsit. A gadget. A toy.'

'And where is your world?' asked Mum.

The Something's golden eyes went dreamy and it fluttered its batwings. 'At the other end of nowhere, under the rim of the Earth.'

CHAPTER THREE

'The Earth's not flat,' argued Dad. 'And it doesn't have a rim.'

'Does.'

'Doesn't.'

'Does! Does! Does!'

'Let's not quarrel,' said Mum quickly. 'Just tell us what you are and what you live on. If you're going to be our guest, we really ought to know.'

'I'm a whippersnapper!' sang the Something, grabbing a fresh sheet of kitchen roll. 'And I live on paper and printer's ink.'

'Well, I'm a boy,' Jamie told them. 'And I'm still hungry.'

He goggled as Mum broke the three duck eggs into a bowl. 'I'll scramble these,' she said. 'We can have them on toast.'

She whisked the eggs and cooked

them with butter.

'They taste funny,' grumbled Jamie.

'They're delicious!' exclaimed Dad.

The whippersnapper offered Jamie some kitchen roll. 'It's rustly and tickly and papery and nice. Try some,' it told him.

But Jamie pulled a face. 'I don't eat paper.'

'Then you don't know what you're missing,' the whippersnapper cried.

'I just want something ordinary,' argued Jamie. 'Like supermarket eggs.'

The whippersnapper sniffed. 'Never satisfied, are you?'

Dad switched on the TV, showing off. 'Look. That's the big match,' he told the whippersnapper. 'Bet your rotten old magic's got nothing like that.'

But the footballers kept turning into pink pigs in shorts.

'I prefer them that way,' laughed Mum, opening a can of beans for Jamie.

'Oh, bother,' muttered Dad, fiddling with the knobs.

Then the whippersnapper's golden eyes glittered and shone. 'TV, TV,' it squealed. 'Another whirligig. The really good pictures are inside your head.'

Dad said a bad word and tried another channel, where the News was read by a crocodile in a yellow silk shirt.

'I like his tie,' murmured Mum. 'But he looks silly in glasses.'

'I give up!' exploded Dad, and he glowered at the whippersnapper. 'I wish we *had* boiled you! I wish you'd get lost!'

'Wicked!' The whippersnapper swung from the light flex. 'But you haven't got the power to lose me, so your wishes won't work.'

'You mean, *someone* has got the power?' cried Mum.

'He has, of course.' The whippersnapper pointed at Jamie. 'Because he's the one who called me.'

'No I didn't,' Jamie yelled.

'You made a sky,' wailed the whippersnapper. 'A big purple sky, and a castle, and a wizard and a witch. You wished magic was real, so I came through.' Its eyes swam with golden tears. 'But now you don't want me!'

The tears plopped on to Jamie's baked beans and made bouncy bubbles in Mum's cup of tea. 'I'll go if you don't want me,' howled the whippersnapper.

'The sooner, the better!' shouted Dad.

'Of course we want you,' whispered Jamie. 'But please,' he begged, 'let my dad watch his match. He'll be grumpy and cross if he misses it.'

CHAPTER FOUR

'Bedtime,' announced Mum at half past eight.

'If you say so, lady.' The whipper-snapper nuzzled Jamie's ear. 'Come on, boy. Let's go.'

'Not you,' said Mum firmly.

'Oh, please,' Jamie begged.

'I can't leave Jamie,' said the whippersnapper. 'He called me. He's mine.'

'You're not sleeping in Jamie's room,' Mum said firmly.

Jamie grabbed a piece of string and dangled it over her shoulders. 'I could ask it for a worm . . .' he teased, '. . . to go wriggly-wriggly-wriggly . . .'

'Don't do that!' Mum shuddered. 'And the answer's still no.' Jamie wriggled his string. 'Oh well, maybe,' she faltered.

Then Jamie grinned triumphantly.

'Thanks, Mum,' he said. 'And I'll be OK, honest.'

He kissed Dad goodnight, but Dad didn't really notice. He never did when he was watching something on TV.

Mum followed them upstairs. 'I'm leaving your door open,' she told Jamie, 'in case there's trouble in the night.'

'If there's trouble,' said the whipper-snapper, dangling from the picture rail, 'I'll handle it, lady. You don't have to do a thing.'

'I think she meant you,' Jamie told it
after Mum had left,

'I'm not trouble,' the whippersnapper
cried indignantly. 'What would I do?'

'Magic,' breathed Jamie. 'Come on.
Show me.'

'You've got to sleep.'

'Oh, please?' Jamie begged.

Then the whippersnapper's eyes
glittered golden and bright, and Jamie
floated up and sailed out through the
window.

At first he was terrified. 'I'm falling!' he yelled.

'Never!' cried the whippersnapper. 'Not when you're with me.'

Gradually Jamie began to feel safer. This wasn't so different from learning to swim. At last, when a cool breeze blew across his face, he just spread out his arms. 'Wow! I'm flying!' he sang.

'*We're* flying, if you please,' the whippersnapper corrected.

They flew over the gasworks and the big supermarket. They flew over the roads and out to the hills.

They dived into a forest where fox cubs were playing. They saw badgers out snuffling, and hedgehogs and owls.

They flew down to the river where otters splashed about in the moonlight. Jamie crouched down to watch them. They seemed very tame.

'Can they see us?' he asked.

'Of course not, silly!'

'It's like an animal programme on TV,' Jamie exclaimed. 'Except it's real. Oh, I could stay here for ever.'

'Too bad,' said the whippersnapper, and Jamie suddenly found himself back in the air.

'Home time,' called the whipper-snapper from his shoulder.

'Not yet,' grumbled Jamie.

'School tomorrow,' said the whipper-snapper.

'Hey! How did you know?' Jamie gasped.

CHAPTER FIVE

Next morning, Mum looked anxiously at Jamie. 'Did you sleep well?' she asked. Then she tore off some kitchen roll and put it on a plate. 'For you,' she told the whippersnapper.

But, 'I want what he's having,' the whippersnapper said.

So Mum shook out another bowl of rice crispies,

'Crackle! Munch! Pop!' went the whippersnapper. 'What a great noise!'

'All this silly nonsense!' Dad complained. He picked up his briefcase and pointed at the clock. 'I'm already late for the office,' he growled. 'And you'll be late for school.'

Jamie put on his coat and the whippersnapper settled on his shoulder. It rustled its silken batwings. 'I'm ready!' it announced.

'Not you,' said Dad. 'You're not going to school.'

The whippersnapper gave an impatient sigh. 'I keep telling you,' it said. 'I can't leave Jamie. He called me. He's mine.'

'Well that's too bad,' said Dad.

Mum went outside to start the car. The engine snorted, coughed, then died.

'Another whirligig?' teased the whipper-snapper.

Dad's face went pink. I forgot to buy petrol,' he said.

'No problem,' squealed the whipper-snapper. 'I'll take Jamie to school.'

'Oh no you won't!' yelled Mum, but they'd already vanished, and when she ran outside, she could see nothing but a small black dot that quickly vanished in the clouds.

In the playground, Jamie's friend, Mike, was dribbling a football. When Jamie suddenly appeared, he jumped in the air. 'Hey, where did you come from?'

Jamie grinned. 'From the other end of nowhere!'

'No you didn't. That's me,' the whippersnapper said.

'It can talk?' muttered Mike. 'That thing on your shoulder!'

'I talk better sense than you lot!' the whippersnapper huffed.

Mrs Evans blew the whistle. 'Line up!' she called. Then, 'Whatever's that?' she exclaimed as Jamie walked past her.

'I'm a whippersnapper, lady,' the

whippersnapper told her.

'Well you can't come into school,' Mrs Evans said.

'But I can't leave Jamie. He called me. He's mine.'

'Too bad,' snapped Mrs Evans. 'You'll have to wait in the playground. It's a school rule – no pets in the classroom.'

Then the whippersnapper's eyes flashed like two halogen bulbs. 'No hens either,' it snapped.

And Mrs Evans turned into a chicken with glasses. 'Cackle, coo,' she complained, strutting about.

People pointed and giggled. 'Hey, look at that chicken! It looks a bit like Mrs Evans!'

'Change her back,' whispered Jamie. 'She's OK really. She's nice.'

'Cackle, coo, oh!' gasped Mrs Evans, adjusting her glasses. Then she peered at the whippersnapper. 'I suppose you don't count as a pet,' she said weakly. 'But if I let you in, you'll have to behave.'

'Don't worry, miss,' Jamie told her. 'I'll see to that.'

CHAPTER SIX

The school secretary came running into the classroom.

'Is Jamie Travers here?' she huffed. 'Because his mum wants to know.'

'Hey, where does she think you are?' people joked.

'On the other side of nowhere,' giggled Jamie.

The secretary suddenly shrieked, 'A-a-h!' and backed off hurriedly. 'What's that thing on your shoulder?' she screamed.

The whippersnapper yawned. 'I'm a whippersnapper, lady.' But the secretary was already halfway down the hall.

'Enough messing around,' said Mrs Evans. She handed out some books. 'Let's get down to work.'

The whippersnapper licked its lips with its little golden tongue.

'Watch it,' Jamie whispered. 'No paper eating.'

'But those pages look so scrumptious!'

'Just be good,' Jamie said.

Everyone jostled, trying to get close.

'What's that on your shoulder?' people asked.

'It's a flying mouse,' said a girl.

'It's an alien!'

'It's a Batman puppet,' said a boy. 'And it's Jamie doing the talking.'

But the whippersnapper'd heard enough. 'Oh, piddlesticks!' it cried.

After dinner, Mike, Jamie and the gang went outside with Mike's football. The dinner lady who always picked on them prowled around, watching. She didn't approve of boys, especially ones who brought in footballs.

Someone kicked the ball and Mike headed it, sending it over the railings and into the field.

Ben, the skinniest boy in Jamie's class, wriggled through and lobbed it over.

The dinner lady frowned. '*Boys*,' she thought. 'As usual, up to no good . . .'

Mike pointed at Jamie. 'Can you still play with that bat thing sitting on your shoulder?'

'You mean my whippersnapper?' said Jamie airily. 'You bet I can. Watch this!' And he kicked the ball higher than he'd ever kicked before. He kicked it – crash! – right through a second floor window.

The dinner lady came running. She'd been expecting something like this. She stood over Jamie, looking very angry.

'Big trouble for you, my lad!' she yelled. 'Your dad's going to have to pay for that window!'

CHAPTER SEVEN

Jamie just stood there, going pink and wobbly. Mum would be mad with him and Dad would go bananas! There'd be no pocket money for years until that window was paid for.

Then Mrs Evans rushed out, holding the ball.

'Nothing's broken!' She laughed weakly. 'Can't understand it. We all heard the glass splinter, and then this ball appeared. But there's no hole in the glass. Seems like some kind of magic . . .' Then she frowned at the boys. 'But I'm keeping this,' she told them. 'You know the rules. No goalie kicks in the playground. Oh if only Mr Biggins would let us buy that old field . . .' she sighed.

Mike nodded. 'If we cleared up all the junk, it would make a great football pitch.'

'We could have Sports Day there,' added Jamie. 'And super picnics . . .'

Mrs Evans smiled. 'Well, if wishes were horses,' she told them, 'beggars would ride.'

At the end of the afternoon, Jamie waited in the playground for Mum. She was late that day, and most people had left.

'I could take us home,' grumbled the whippersnapper.

'But then Mum would turn up and not find us. And she'd be really worried. And that wouldn't be fair.' He spotted the Fiesta. 'Anyway, there she is.'

The whippersnapper tittered. 'In that blue whirligig with wheels?'

'Listen, I like our car,' Jamie told it.

That evening, their TV showed green mice on ice skates, and the News was read by a guinea pig in a bikini.

'Her earrings are quite trendy,' mused Mum. 'But that straw hat doesn't suit her.'

Dad's face turned purple. He pointed a quivering finger at the screen. 'This is your fault!' he roared at the whipper-snapper. 'You and your rotten old magic! I wish we had boiled you!'

'Oh, nobody likes me,' the whipper-snapper wailed.

'Calm down,' ordered Mum. She put rice crispies and kitchen roll into a bowl, but the whippersnapper still sulked, puffing out sad grey smoke rings.

'If our TV's gone funny,' Mum said, 'we'll have to do something else, won't we?' She rifled through a drawer and pulled out a gameboard. 'Snakes and Ladders,' she announced. 'It's ages since we all played a game together.'

She brought in cans of beer for her and Dad, and a fizzy drink for Jamie. She found a mixed packet of crisps. 'Cheese and pickle,' she read, choosing a small bag. 'Nice and noisy.' She gave it to the whippersnapper. 'You can eat the bag, too.' Then she rolled the dice for six. 'Look, I've started,' she told them.

'Oh, no!' wailed Jamie as a snake swallowed his counter. The snake wriggled sideways and gobbled up Dad's piece instead.

'See? That's magic!' crowed the whippersnapper. 'I can fix things so you'll win.'

But Jamie frowned. 'That's not fair,' he said.

The whippersnapper drooped. 'It's fair if I say so,' it muttered.

'No, it isn't,' Jamie told it.

'You don't like my magic,' the whippersnapper complained, but Jamie was too busy playing to notice.

They played seven games without magic, but Dad still didn't win any.

'We'll have to play again tomorrow.' He finished up his beer. 'Then I'll beat you two hollow!'

'If we let you!' And Jamie grinned.

CHAPTER EIGHT

Puffs of sad grey smoke rose
from Jamie's dressing
gown pocket.

'You're sulking,'
said Jamie.

'No I'm not,'
grumped the
whippersnapper.

'Oh stop it,'
said Jamie. 'And come out of there.'

The whippersnapper fluttered
mournfully on to his pillow and wrapped
its batwings around its head.

'Cheer up,' Jamie told it. 'Let's do
something good. Where shall we go?'

'Nowhere,' growled the whippersnapper. 'You don't like me. You said
magic's cheating.'

'Of course I like you.' Jamie stroked

its rainbow tummy. 'And magic's only cheating sometimes . . .'

'Anyway,' said the whippersnapper, 'boys have to sleep.'

'I won't be able to sleep,' Jamie told it. 'I'll be too disappointed.'

'OK,' sighed the whippersnapper. 'If you say so. You called me.' So they rose out of the window and flew over the town.

They flew beyond the football pitch and the shopping centre and the dark, damp fields where sheep stood huddled. And they flew over cities and motorways and hills. Then they came to an island where the ocean rose silver, and seals lay basking on wet, starlit rocks.

Jamie watched. 'Can I stroke one?'

'It wouldn't work.'

'Can I paddle in the sea, then?'

'Looking, not touching,' the whippersnapper told him primly. 'Anyway, it's time you were back in bed.'

'We've run out of milk,' wailed Mum at breakfast.

'That's OK,' crunched the whippersnapper. 'I prefer my crispies dry.'

Mum pulled a face. 'But I don't fancy tea without milk.'

'Magic?' whispered Jamie. 'It's OK this time.'

And suddenly there, in the kitchen, stood a black and white cow.

'Oh, no!' shouted Mum, but Dad just grinned.

'Jamie,' he called. 'Go and fetch a clean bowl.'

Then Dad sat astride a kitchen stool and began to milk the cow. 'After all, I did grow up on a farm,' he said. 'So I should know how.'

They had fresh milk on their crispies. Mum had fresh milk in her tea.

Suddenly they all held their noses.

'Cow pats!' groaned Mum. 'All over my nice clean floor.'

'I'll sort out the cow pats,' offered Dad. 'I'll sort out the cow, too. You get Jamie to school!'

'That's my job!' said the whipper-snapper.

'Oh dear, they've gone again,' blinked Mum.

'But so have the cow pats.' Dad suddenly hugged her and danced her around. 'And look,' he pointed. 'So has the cow!'

CHAPTER NINE

In the playground, Mrs Evans dropped all her papers.

'Jamie Travers!' she exclaimed. 'Where on earth did you come from?'

'Sorry,' said Jamie. 'I didn't mean to scare you.' He helped her to pick up her things and pack them away.

Mrs Evans stared at the whipper-snapper.

'It's a very odd pet,' she said as they went inside. 'It terrified the secretary. I'm still not at all sure we should let you bring it in.'

Then the whippersnapper cackled like a chicken and turned a cartwheel in the air. 'You've got no choice, lady,' it pointed out.

'Miss, can I have my ball back?' pleaded Mike in the classroom.

'With a promise.' Mrs Evans suddenly

looked fierce. 'No more goalie kicks in our little playground. You know the rules. You nearly broke a window.'

'That was me,' put in Jamie. 'It wasn't him.'

'We could have had a proper game in that old field,' grumbled Mike. 'Some of us get in there already. It's easy-peasy to squeeze through those bent railings . . .'

Mrs Evans frowned. 'I didn't hear that.'

'So why can't we play in there? No one wants it.'

'The school's trying to buy it,' explained Mrs Evans. 'But Mr Biggins wants to sell it to developers. That way he gets more money.'

'What a meanie!' they groaned.

'Well, the land is his,' Mrs Evans pointed out.

'I want to go home,' sighed the whippersnapper after dinner. 'Your world's too full of whirligigs,' he said looking at the school computers. 'There's not much room for magic.' It lolled against Jamie's neck and blew out more sad grey smoke rings.

'You got a firework?' someone called out.

'Bet it's a banger,' said a girl, covering her ears.

Mike came over and peered. 'Hey, your pet's smoking!'

'It's just sad,' explained Jamie. 'It says it wants to go home.'

'Where is its home?' asked Mike.

'On the other side of nowhere.'

Mike dribbled his football. 'Where's that supposed to be?'

The dinner lady charged across. She made a grab for Jamie and Mike. 'You two again?' she shouted. 'Can't keep out of trouble, can you? Broken windows yesterday and fireworks today. Or could it be a cigarette? Quack!' she squawked. 'Quack, quack, qua-a-rk!' she yelped crossly, stamping away on orange webbed feet.

Mike's mouth dropped open. 'Where did the dinner lady go?' He grabbed Jamie and pointed. 'And look, there's a silly fat duck!'

'Hey, there's a duck in the play-ground!' people yelled, trying to catch it.

Jamie grinned. 'Keep her that way,' he whispered to the whippersnapper. 'At least till going-home time. She's always picking on us, and she always thinks she's right . . .'

CHAPTER TEN

Mum picked up Jamie after school.
'Oh, look,' she pointed. 'There's a duck
in your playground. Oh, it's gone!'

The dinner lady shook herself and
glowered, then marched crossly into
school.

'Where on earth did that duck go?'
wondered Mum.

That night, Dad came home with a pizza
and a newspaper. He spread the paper
out for the whippersnapper. 'It's an old
one,' he said. 'So it's all yours.'

'M-m-m,' purred the whippersnapper.
'Thank you,' it said. 'I'll start with the ads
and then I'll nibble the pictures. The
stories are the best bits, so I'll leave
those till last . . .'

The News that night was read by a
tortoise, who took so long about it that

they had to switch him off.

'I liked his silver nose rings,' murmured Mum, 'but not that baseball cap . . .'

'Enough nonsense!' cried Dad. 'Snakes and Ladders, anyone?'

Mum grinned, then winked at Jamie. 'OK,' she said.

Dad won twice that night.

'Said I would,' he boasted, but nobody minded.

At last Mum packed away the board. 'Bedtime,' she said.

'Oh, no,' grumbled Jamie.

Dad gave him a bear hug.

'Hey, watch out for me!' huffed the whippersnapper from Jamie's shoulder.

Upstairs, Jamie waited for Mum to kiss him goodnight and for the whipper-snapper to stop sniffing at the books on his shelf.

'Will you take me to the other side of nowhere?' Jamie asked it.

The whippersnapper blinked. 'I only wish I could.'

'The moon, then,' breathed Jamie.

'I don't care for cheeses.'

'Silly!' Jamie laughed. 'The moon's not made of cheese.'

'Is!'

'No it isn't. It's rocks and craters and things.'

'The moon's a big round cheese with holes in it,' insisted the whippersnapper.

'If you say so,' sighed Jamie. 'So where shall we go?'

The whippersnapper tucked itself inside its batwings. 'To sleep,' it said. 'I'm really very tired.'

'Oh, who wants to sleep?' yawned Jamie.

CHAPTER ELEVEN

'You snored,' complained Jamie.

'Didn't.'

'Yes you did! I heard you.'

'Stop squabbling, you two.' Mum shook out rice crispies for the whippersnapper. 'Will you take Jamie this morning?' she asked it. 'I've got shopping to do.'

'Mr Biggins is coming today,' Mrs Evans told the class.

'To our school?' they all gasped.

And Mrs Evans nodded. 'We've asked him to open the new Infants' annexe.'

People groaned.

'Why not a footballer?' Mike shouted. 'Or a pop star? Or someone from TV?'

'We want to be nice to Mr Biggins.' Mrs Evans winked. 'Don't we? Then perhaps he'll change his mind about that old field.'

So at half past two, they all assembled in

the playground.

The headteacher came out, followed by a fat little man and a large snooty lady in a big feather hat.

Someone had taped some orange ribbon across the annexe door. Then the fat little man was given a large pair of scissors.

'Children, this is Mr Biggins,' announced the Head, and they wriggled and giggled and clapped politely.

The lady glared. 'Haven't you forgotten someone?'

'And Mrs Biggins, his charming wife,' the Head added hastily. 'My apologies, madam.'

'I should think so, too,' Mrs Biggins sniffed. Then she nudged the little fat man. 'So get on with it, Biggins!'

Mr Biggins cleared this throat, fiddled with the scissors and droned on and on and on.

The infants grew restless. They pulled each other's hair and Maisie Parker in the front row began picking her nose.

'This is so boring,' Jamie whispered to the whippersnapper. 'Can't you do something?'

The whippersnapper examined the tips of its small sugar-pink fingers. 'Magic's cheating,' it said. 'You said so.'

'Only in games and things – I told you.' Jamie fondled its wings. 'Listen, I

think magic's great! That cow in our
kitchen really cheered up my dad, and our
dinner lady's much nicer since that time
she was a duck.'

The whippersnapper nuzzled Jamie's
ear. Then it flashed its golden eyes.

And, 'Eeek!' cried Mrs Biggins as she
turned into an ostrich. Then she stuck
her head in the sandpit and waggled her
bottom in the air.

'Chatter-chatter-chatter . . .' Mr Biggins
swung from the railings.
Then he hooked his brown
monkey's tail around the
gate post. 'Chatter-
chatter-wow!' he called,
hanging upside down.

The infants loved
it! 'More!' they
squealed. 'More!'

Mr Biggins
scratched his

armpits and gobbled up a flea. He did handstands and cartwheels and tried on Miss Thomas's mauve felt hat.

They were all still clapping and cheering when Mr Biggins changed back.

'More!' yelled the infants.

Mr Biggins went pink. Then he handed back the felt hat. 'Sorry,' he croaked.

'Oh don't be.' Miss Thomas gave him a dazzling smile. 'You were so funny! You were really great!'

Mr Biggins blinked shyly. 'I've never made anyone laugh before. I mean, not on purpose . . .'

'A disgraceful performance!' Mrs Biggins spat out sand and smoothed down her skirt. 'Biggins!' she bellowed. 'Pull yourself together!'

Then Mr Biggins stood on tiptoe and glared at Mrs Biggins.

'Be quiet, Mrs Biggins!' Mr Biggins said firmly. 'Can't you see that I'm

talking to all these nice people?' He
picked up the scissors and snipped the
orange ribbon.

'I now declare,' he announced, 'that
the annexe is open.' He scratched his
armpits again and waggled his fingers
and did a little dance so that everyone
laughed. 'And who knows?' he added
thoughtfully, 'I might even join a circus
and learn to be a clown . . .'

CHAPTER TWELVE

'We're getting that field,' Jamie told Mum a few days later. 'My whippersnapper fixed it.'

'Mrs Evans helped,' squeaked the whippersnapper from Jamie's shoulder. 'It wasn't just me.'

Jamie held up his crisp bag. 'Listen, you're the best!'

'That old dump will need a bit of clearing,' Mum observed.

Jamie nodded. 'I've brought home a letter about that.' He handed it to Mum. 'The school wants people to help at the weekend . . . parents and things . . .' He looked hopefully at Dad who was usually too busy.

Dad looked at the letter. Then he grinned and flexed his muscles. 'How about it, Jamie?' he said. 'Sounds like a good day's work for us two blokes!'

That night, the News was read by a man in a grey striped suit and a red and blue tie.

'Now that makes more sense!' Dad said, settling down to watch.

'It's not the same, though,' sighed Mum.

'Fancy a story later on?' Dad asked.

'You bet,' Jamie said.

'A story.' The whippersnapper sounded quite disappointed. 'Then you won't be needing me.' But no one seemed to hear.

Dad read Jamie three stories. Jamie wanted more. He didn't notice that the whippersnapper wasn't on his shoulder. Dad did, though. 'Where's your little friend?' he asked.

'The whippersnapper went up to Jamie's room,' said Mum. 'It seemed to be tired.'

Upstairs, Jamie found the whipper-snapper drooping miserably over a cushion, sighing out pale floppy rings of sad grey smoke.

Jamie stroked its folded wings with the tip of one finger. 'You're so sad,' he said. 'Why don't we go somewhere? It might make you feel better.'

But the whippersnapper was silent.

'All your wishes have come true,' it said at last.

Jamie thought about that. 'I suppose they have,' he said.

The whippersnapper uncurled.
Golden tears rolled down its shiny black
snout and hung like shiny beads on its
rainbow tummy. 'So send me home,' it
wept.

Jamie was shocked. 'But I don't want
to. And anyway, I don't know how.'

'You don't?' bristled the whippersnapper, shaking its wings. 'But it was
you who called me!'

'I still don't know how,' argued Jamie.

'You lot aren't very bright, are you?'
The whippersnapper sighed. 'I'll have to
show you. Unpin your magic castle
picture and lay it flat.' Jamie did as it
told him. 'Now wish,' it ordered Jamie.
'Wish for me to go.'

But Jamie shook his head. 'Can't.'

'Please,' begged the whippersnapper.

Jamie made himself say it. 'I wish
you'd go,' he mumbled.

'You've got to mean it,' said the

whippersnapper. 'Or it won't work.'

'I wish you'd go!' yelled Jamie, crying, and the whippersnapper went.

There was a crackle and a ping, and an egg lay on the paper, just like one of the duck eggs Mum had brought home. Then a snap and a sizzle, and suddenly nothing at all but a big purple sky with a castle and a witch.

Jamie cried himself to sleep. He would never forget his whippersnapper. But in the middle of the night, he woke up and remembered something nice. At the weekend, he and Dad were going to help clear out that old field. Jamie smiled and snuggled down happily.

'Thank you, Whippersnapper,' he whispered.